This book has been
donated by Dover, PA
Intermediate School
students in homeroom 11
in celebration of
Dr. Seuss's birthday for
Read Across America.
March 2, 2006

Enjoy Reading!

The Month-Brothers

✦ A SLAVIC TALE ✦

Retold by Samuel Marshak
Translation from the Russian by Thomas P. Whitney

Illustrated by Diane Stanley

Morrow Junior Books
New York

to Jenny and James

T.P.W.

for John Leslie,
who brightens every month
of the year

D.S.

Printed in the United States of America.

4 5 6 7 8 9 10 11 12 13

Library of Congress Cataloging in Publication Data
Marshak, S. (Samuil), 1887–1964. The Month-Brothers.
Translation of: Dvenadtsat' mesiatsev. Summary: A retelling of the Slavic folktale in which a young girl outwits her greedy stepmother and stepsister with the help of the Month Brothers who use their magic to enable her to fulfill seemingly impossible tasks. [1. Folklore—Slavic countries] I. Whitney, Thomas P. II. Stanley, Diane, ill. III. Title.
PZ8.1.M3535Mo 1983   398.2′1′0947 [E] 82-7927 AACR2
ISBN 0-688-01509-3
ISBN 0-688-01510-7 (lib. bdg.)

T 68678

Do you know how many months are in a year?
Twelve.

And what are they named?

January, February, March, April, May, June, July, August, September, October, November, December.

Just as soon as one month comes to an end, another commences. And never has it happened that February has come before January or May before April. The months follow one another and never meet.

But people tell how once upon a time in the mountainous land of Bohemia there was a little girl who saw all twelve months at once. How could this have happened?

Here is how it was.

In a certain tiny village lived a wicked, stingy woman with her daughter and a stepdaughter. She loved her daughter, but her stepdaughter could do nothing to suit her. Everything the stepdaughter did was wrong.

The daughter used to loll about the whole day long on her featherbed devouring sweetmeats, while the stepdaughter never got a chance to rest from morn till night. She had to haul water, bring firewood from the forest, do the laundry in the stream, weed the beds in the garden.

She knew well the cold of winter and the heat of summer, the winds of spring and the rains of the autumn. And that, you might say, is how she once got to see all the twelve months at one time.

It was winter. It was January. There were such deep snowfalls that the snow had to be shoveled away from in front of the doors. And out in the forest the trees were so deeply buried in drifts that they could not even sway in the wind. People stayed indoors and kept the fires in their stoves burning.

One time toward dusk the wicked stepmother opened the door a bit and watched the blizzard outside. Then she went back to the stove and said to her stepdaughter, "Go on out into the woods and pick some snowdrops. Tomorrow is your sister's birthday."

The little girl looked at her stepmother in bewilderment. Was she joking or was she really sending her out into the forest? It was awful out in the woods! And how could you ever find snowdrops there now anyway? You couldn't find them until March no matter how hard you looked. The only thing that could happen to you was that you would get lost in the woods and stuck in the snowdrifts.

And her stepsister said to her, "So what if you do get lost out there! No one is going to shed any tears over you anyway! Be off with you, and don't come home without the flowers. Here's a basket for you to take."

Weeping, the little girl wrapped herself in a tattered shawl and went outside.

The snow blown by the wind stung her eyes and kept trying to tear her shawl away from her. She marched ahead just barely able to move through the deep drifts.

Everything grew dark. The heavens were black, and not a single star could be seen. But things were a bit lighter on the ground—because of the white snow.

She entered the forest, and there it was completely black; she couldn't see her hands in front of her face. The little girl sat down on a fallen tree and thought to herself, It doesn't make any difference where I freeze.

But suddenly, far off, a light gleamed from between the trees—like a star caught in the branches.

The girl got up and went in the direction of the light. She kept struggling through the drifts and clambering over fallen timber.

"Oh, I do hope," she said to herself, "that the light doesn't go out."

Indeed it did not go out. It kept shining ever more brightly. There was a smell of warm smoke in the air, and she could hear firewood crackling in a fire.

The little girl quickened her stride and emerged into a clearing. And there she came to a startled halt.

The clearing was bright, bright like sunlight. In the middle of it a big bonfire was burning, and its flames leaped upward nearly to the sky. Around the bonfire men were seated, some close to the fire and some farther back. They were sitting there and conversing quietly.

The little girl gazed at them and wondered who they were. They did not look like hunters. Even less did they look like woodcutters. They were all beautifully dressed—some in silver, some in gold, some in green velvet.

She began to count them, and there were twelve. Three were old, three were of middle age, three were young. And the remaining three were mere boys.

The young ones sat right near the fire. The old ones sat the farthest away from it.

All of a sudden one old man—the tallest, with a beard and with bushy eyebrows—turned about and looked at the little girl.

She was frightened and wanted to run away, but it was too late. The old man asked loudly, "Where are you from? What do you want here?"

The little girl showed him her empty basket and said, "I have to fill this basket with snowdrops."

The old man laughed. "Snowdrops in January? You must be crazy!"

"It wasn't my idea," the little girl replied. "It was my stepmother who sent me here to pick snowdrops and who told me not to come home with an empty basket."

Then and there all twelve looked at her and began to talk with each other.

The little girl stood there and listened, but she did not understand their words, which were like the sound of the wind in the leaves. They talked and talked and then fell silent.

And the tall old man once again turned to the little girl and asked, "What will happen to you if you don't find snowdrops? After all, they don't appear until March."

"I will stay in the forest," said the little girl. "I will wait for the month of March. It's better to freeze in the woods than to return home without snowdrops." She started sobbing.

Then all of a sudden, the youngest of the twelve, a jolly chap with a sheepskin jacket over one shoulder, got up and went over to the old man. "Brother January, let me take your place for just an hour!"

The old man stroked his long beard and said, "I would let you take my place, but you can't have March coming before February."

"Oh, all right," muttered another old man, all shaggy and possessing a disheveled beard. "Go ahead and let him take your place. I'm not going to object! We all know her very well; we have run into her at the ice hole with buckets and in the woods with bundles of firewood. She belongs to all us months. We have to help her now."

"Well, so be it," said January.

He knocked with his icy crook and chanted:

"Do not crackle, frosts,
in the primeval forest!
Do not gnaw the bark
of the pines and birches!
Enough of freezing
flocks of crows!
And chilling
human dwellings!"

The old man fell silent, and things grew quiet in the forest. The trees stopped crackling from the frosts, and snow fell densely in large, soft clumps.

"Well, now it's your turn, brother," said January, and he gave the crook to his smaller brother, shaggy February.

February in his turn knocked with the crook, shook his beard, and shrilled:

"Winds, storms, hurricanes,
blow your very worst!
Blizzards, gales, and tempests,
blow until you burst!
Trumpet loudly in the clouds,
hover over the earth!
And through the fields let a ground wind twist,
like a white snake!"

And just as soon as he had spoken, a stormy, wet wind howled through the branches. Snow clumps whirled in the air, and white gales stormed over the earth.

Then February gave his icy crook to his younger brother and said, "Now it's your turn, brother March."

The younger brother took the crook and struck the earth.

The girl watched and saw it was no longer an icy crook. It was a big branch covered with buds.

March laughed and sang out resoundingly with all the strength of his boyish voice:

"Run, streams, run!
Flow, puddles, flow!
Come out, ants, come,
the winter freeze is over!
The bear makes his way
through the forest thickets.
The birds sing their songs
and the snowdrops are in blossom!"

The little girl spread her arms in astonishment. Where had the deep drifts gone? Where had the icicles hanging from each branch gone?

Beneath her feet lay the soft earth of early spring. All about her she heard the sounds of dripping, flowing, gurgling. The buds on the branches were swelling, and the first little green leaves were already peering out from under the dark carpet of leaves.

The little girl kept staring about and could not get her fill.

"What are you standing there for?" March asked her. "You'd better hurry! My brothers made a gift to us of just one hour."

The little girl started. She ran into the grove to look for snowdrops. And they were all over! Beneath the bushes and under stones. On stumps and under stumps. Every place she looked. She picked a basketful and filled her apron too, and soon she returned to the clearing where the bonfire had been burning, where the twelve brothers had been sitting.

But now there was no bonfire, and there were no broth-ers. The clearing was bright—but not as before. The light came not from a bonfire but from a full moon that had risen over the forest.

The little girl felt sorry that there was no one to thank. She ran home, and the full moon floated behind her.

She ran so swiftly she could not even feel her legs beneath her. She ran right up to her own door, and the moment she got indoors once again, the winter blizzard howled outside and the moon hid behind clouds.

"Well, well!" exclaimed the stepmother and her daughter. "So you've come home? But where are the snowdrops?"

The little girl did not utter a word in reply. She merely poured the snowdrops from her apron onto the table and put the basket alongside it.

The stepmother and her daughter exclaimed, "Where did you ever find them?"

The little girl told them exactly what had happened to her. They both listened and kept shaking their heads. They didn't know whether to believe her or not. It was hard to believe her, but right there on the table lay a whole pile of snowdrops, fresh and light blue. And from them wafted the smell of March.

The mother and her daughter looked at one another and asked her, "Did the months give you anything else?"

"I didn't ask them for anything else."

"What a little fool you are!" said the sister. "You had the good luck to meet all the twelve months, and you didn't ask them for anything except snowdrops! Now if I had been in your place, I would have known what to ask for. I would have asked one of them for sweet apples and pears. I would have asked another for ripe strawberries and another still for mushrooms and still another for cucumbers!"

"You're very clever, daughter dear!" said the stepmother. "Strawberries and pears could bring any price at all in wintertime. We could have sold them and made much money! And that little fool brought home a bunch of snowdrops! Get dressed as warmly as you can, daughter, and go to that clearing. They won't outsmart *you*, even though there are twelve of them and one of you."

"Certainly not!" the daughter replied, and she wrapped her shawl about her head and pushed her arms into her coat sleeves.

Her mother shouted after her, "Put on your mittens and button up your coat!"

But the daughter was already out the door and had run off into the forest.

She hurried along, following her sister's tracks. The

sooner I get to the clearing the better, she thought to herself.

The forest kept getting thicker and thicker, darker and darker, and the fallen timbers got higher and higher.

Oh, whew! thought the stepmother's daughter, why did I ever come to the forest! I could be lying down at home on a warm bed, and here I am freezing! And I could die out here too!

No sooner had she had this thought than she saw a light at a distance, just like a star caught in the branches.

She went in the direction of the light. She walked and she walked, and finally she emerged into a clearing. In the middle of the clearing a big bonfire was burning, and around the bonfire sat twelve brothers, the twelve months. They sat there and conversed quietly.

The stepmother's daughter went right up to the bonfire. She did not bow, and she did not utter a word of friendly greeting. She picked the warmest place of all and started to warm herself.

The month-brothers kept their silence. The forest fell silent. And suddenly January knocked with his crook on the ground. "Who may you be?" he asked. "Where did you come from?"

"From home," the stepmother's daughter replied. "Just now you gave my sister a whole basket of snowdrops. And I followed her trail here."

"We know your sister," said January. "But you we have never seen before. Why did you come to us?"

"For some gifts. I want the month of June to pour some strawberries into my basket, and I want them to be large ones too. I want July to give me fresh cucumbers and the very best mushrooms. I want August to give me some apples and sweet pears. From September I want ripe walnuts. And from October..."

"Just wait a minute," said January. "Summer cannot come before spring, nor spring before winter. It's a long time till June. Right now I am master in the forest. And I intend to rule here for thirty-one days."

"What a grouch!" said the stepmother's daughter. "I didn't come to talk to you anyway. There's nothing to be had from you but snow and frost. I need the summer months."

January frowned. "Just you try to find summer in the winter!" he said.

He waved his broad sleeve, and a snowstorm rose from the ground up to the heavens. It wrapped around the trees and the clearing in which the month-brothers were sitting. The bonfire disappeared behind the snowflakes, but the fire could still be heard whistling and crackling somewhere out there.

The stepmother's daughter was frightened. "Stop!" she cried. "That's enough!"

But that made not the least bit of difference. The snowstorm wrapped itself around her, blinded her eyes, stopped up her breath. She fell into a drift and the snow covered her over.

The stepmother kept waiting and waiting for her daughter. She kept looking out the window and running to the door. But the daughter did not come. So the stepmother dressed herself up warmly and went into the forest. What chance was there of finding anyone in a thicket in such a snowstorm and in darkness!

She walked and walked and searched and searched until she herself froze.

And that's how the both of them remained in the forest to wait for the summer.

But the stepdaughter lived a long life. She grew up and got married and raised a family.

And people say that she had about her house a garden more wonderful than anything you have seen. In it the flowers bloomed, the berries and apples and pears ripened before anyplace else. When elsewhere it was hot, there it was cool. And when elsewhere there was a snowstorm, there things were quiet.

And people used to say, "That woman has all the months of the year as her guests."

And who knows? Maybe that is how it was.

About This Story

The Month-Brothers is a retelling by Samuel Marshak in his own words of a folktale of the Slavic peoples of Czechoslovakia, which like many folktales appears in other versions in other folk cultures. That is why this tale is set in Bohemia, another name for a portion of modern-day Czechoslovakia. Marshak made use of this story as well, along with much other folktale material, in a children's play entitled *The Twelve Months* published in Moscow during World War II and performed at the Moscow Art Theater. The young reader is certain to notice in *The Month-Brothers* one particular facet of this story that at first glance seems unusual. In it the months of January and February are the "old men," whereas the month of March is "the youngest of all." This description reflects the folk concept of rural people, living in a very cold clime, of a year beginning not on January 1 according to a formal calendar, but in March when nature begins to come to life again after the frigid "old age" of winter has started to end.